The New York Times Best-Selling Series by
Henry Winkler & Lin Oliver

Here's HANK

Always Watch Out for the Flying Potato Salad!

ILLUSTRATED BY SCOTT GARRETT

Penguin Workshop

An Imprint of Penguin Random House

To Stacey always—HW

For Reveta Bowers . . . in appreciation
of all you've done for so many kids—LO

For all the children at Christ Church School,
St Leonards-on-Sea—SG

PENGUIN WORKSHOP
Penguin Young Readers Group
An Imprint of Penguin Random House LLC

Text copyright © 2017 by Henry Winkler and Lin Oliver Productions, Inc.
Illustrations copyright © 2017 by Scott Garrett. All rights reserved.
Published by Penguin Workshop, an imprint of Penguin Random House LLC,
345 Hudson Street, New York, New York 10014. PENGUIN and
PENGUIN WORKSHOP are trademarks of Penguin Books Ltd, and
the W colophon is a trademark of Penguin Random House LLC.
Printed in the USA.

Typeset in Dyslexie Font B.V.
Dyslexie Font B.V. was designed by Christian Boer.

Library of Congress Control Number: 2017932714

ISBN 9781101995839 (pbk)   10 9 8 7 6 5 4 3 2
ISBN 9781101995846 (hc)   10 9 8 7 6 5 4 3 2

The books in the Here's Hank series are designed using the font Dyslexie. A Dutch graphic designer and dyslexic, Christian Boer, developed the font specifically for dyslexic readers. It's designed to make letters more distinct from one another and to keep them tied down, so to speak, so that the readers are less likely to flip them in their minds. The letters in the font are also spaced wide apart to make reading them easier.

Dyslexie has characteristics that make it easier for people with dyslexia to distinguish (and not jumble, invert, or flip) individual letters, such as: heavier bottoms (b, d), larger than normal openings (c, e), and longer ascenders and descenders (f, h, p).

This fun-looking font will help all kids—not just those who are dyslexic— read faster, more easily, and with fewer errors. If you want to know more about the Dyslexie font, please visit the site www.dyslexiefont.com.

CHAPTER 1

"Remember, everyone, tomorrow is Take Your Child to Work Day," Ms. Flowers said to us after recess. "Who's happy about that?"

Before I even thought about it, my hand shot up in the air.

"Would you like to tell us why, Hank?" she asked with that nice smile of hers.

"I'm happy because it means that we won't have a spelling test," I answered. "Which is great for me because I'm having trouble

with the word *window*. I can
only remember the first three
letters, which are W-I-N. Win."

"That's a word that has nothing
to do with you, Zipper Teeth,"
Nick McKelty snarled. "Because
you are a total loser."

"Nick!" Ms. Flowers said.
"We don't insult one another in
this class. Now, tell me what your
plans are for Friday."

"My dad's taking me to work
at his new bowling alley," McKelty
said proudly.

"Are they going to use your head
to knock down the pins?" I asked.

The class laughed. That felt good
to me, but not to Ms. Flowers.

"Hank, did you hear what I

just said to Nick? We don't insult people in this class."

"My brain knows that, but my tongue forgot," I explained.

The class laughed out loud again.

"Well, next time, have a talk with your tongue before you let it loose," she said. I have to admit, Ms. Flowers can be pretty funny herself.

"Anyone else want to share what they're doing for Take Your Child to Work Day?" she asked.

She was kind of looking at me when she asked that.

Please don't call on me, I thought to myself. *Call on anyone else but me. I don't have an answer to that question.*

"Hank," Ms. Flowers asked,

"what are your plans?"

The truth was, I didn't have any yet. I had tried to make plans. Actually, what I made was half a plan. I had asked my dad if I could go with him to work. He said that would be weird, since he works at the dining-room table, which is only about twenty steps from my bedroom. I wouldn't even have to get out of my pajamas.

So then I decided that I would ask my mom if I could go work at her deli, the Crunchy Pickle. But then, as always, my brain forgot to ask her the question.

Ms. Flowers was still standing there, waiting for my answer.

"My plans are a surprise," I said.

What I didn't say was that they
were going to be a surprise even
to me!

"Oh, surprises are such fun,"
she said. "I can't wait to hear all
about it."

You and me both, I thought.

As usual, my best friend Frankie
Townsend jumped in to save me.

"I'm going uptown with my dad
to Columbia University," he said.
"He's a professor
there, and he's going
to let me teach
something to his class."

"How wonderful,"
Ms. Flowers said.
"What are you going to teach?"

"I've decided to show them

how to pull a bunny out of a hat, except I don't have a bunny, so I'm going to use a washcloth."

Everyone laughed, me being the loudest. Frankie always cracks me up.

"And I'm going to the hospital with my mom," my other best friend Ashley Wong chimed in. "She's going to operate on someone."

"I hope she's a doctor," Katie Sperling said. "Otherwise it would be gross."

"Of course she's a doctor," Ashley said.

"If I watched an operation,

I would faint all over the place," Katie said.

"I'm not going to watch," Ashley explained. "They don't let kids in the operating room. I'm going to hang out at the nurses' station and help them deliver lunch trays to the patients."

As everyone shared their plans, my mind was racing to figure out what I could do. Why didn't I ask my mom if I could go with her for Take Your Child to Work Day in the first place? It was such an easy question, but it just slipped out of my mind. My mind doesn't always remember little things. Actually, it has a hard time remembering big things, too. I'm lucky I remember where I live.

"I have a special day planned,

too," Ms. Flowers said, leaning back against her desk with a smile. "Principal Love is giving all the teachers a party. He's calling it a Teacher Appreciation Dinner. We're getting delicious food from the Crunchy Pickle deli."

"Who wants pickles for dinner?" Nick McKelty grumbled.

"That's just the name," I called out. "It's my mom's deli, and it's got all kinds of good food."

"Like pickles on toast," he snickered. "Or French-fried pickles? Or maybe pickle juice with chocolate sauce?"

"Eeewww," everyone in the class said at once. Why is it that Nick McKelty is such a jerk, but can still make me feel so bad?

"My grandpa started the deli," I shot back. "He picked that name because he always has pickles with a sandwich. By the way, they make delicious sandwiches there."

"And I'm certainly looking forward to one," Ms. Flowers said. "Tomorrow is going to be a fun day for all of us."

Maybe not for all of us, I thought. My dad had said no, so that left only my mom. It was her or nothing.

CHAPTER 2

That night at dinner, I waited until dessert to bring up the topic.

"Mom, stay calm," I said as she plopped down a bowl of purple goop in front of me. Whatever was in that bowl was pretending to be pudding, but it didn't fool me. I saw the little chunks of eggplant in there. "I have something to ask you. And here it is. Can I go to work with you tomorrow? It's Take Your Child to Work Day."

"Hank, why did you wait so long to ask me?"

"That's a good question, Mom. And I wish I had an answer. But your answer has to be yes."

"Well, it's a very busy day tomorrow," my mom said. "But you haven't left me much choice. I guess you can come."

"Mom, how come Hank gets to go to work with you and I don't?" my little sister, Emily, demanded.

As usual, Emily had her pet iguana, Katherine, draped around her neck. She was feeding her little bits of a disgusting brown banana, which Katherine was snapping up with her long pink tongue.

"Are you in Ms. Flowers's class?" I asked Emily.

"No," she answered.

"Are you a second-grader?"

"No."

"Is tomorrow Take Your Child to Work Day in your class?"

"No."

"Well then, Emily, you've answered your own question," I said. "Oh, by the way, your lizard is spitting up banana. You might want to change your sweater."

"Come on, Katherine," Emily said. "Mommy's going to wipe off your chin."

Emily stood up and headed toward her bedroom.

"Maybe you haven't noticed," I called after her, "but your overgrown toad doesn't have a chin."

"Hank," my mom said. "That's very hurtful. You know how close Emily and Katherine are."

"I was just saying the truth," I said.

"You know, Hank"—my dad cleared his throat like he was going to make a speech—"when you work in the deli tomorrow, you can't say everything that pops into your mind. You have to be pleasant to the customers. You can't be rude like you were to Emily and Katherine."

"No problem," I assured him. "I'm a people person. I'm never rude to humans. I save that for reptiles."

"Let's talk about what some of your responsibilities will be tomorrow," my mom said. "Would you like to take the customers' orders?"

That seemed exciting and fun, until I realized that I'd have to write down their orders. And that meant spelling. I'm pretty sure I know how to spell "milk." And

I have a shot at spelling "bread" correctly. But "pastrami" . . . no way, José!

"I was thinking, Mom, that something involving cream cheese might be good. I can fill up all those metal pans with different kinds of cream cheese and make cool swirls on top. I could even make a happy face with olives."

"This is a business, Hank, not an art project," my dad grumbled.

"You know what," my mom said, "we don't have to talk about this anymore tonight."

Boy, was I thankful for

that. One of my dad's favorite dinnertime topics is what I did wrong during the day and how I can improve.

"Since tomorrow is so busy," my mom said, "I'm just going to put Carlos in charge of you, Hank." She gave me a big smile. "Don't worry. I know he'll find lots of interesting work for you to do."

That sounded great. I went to bed thinking about all the fun I'd have getting to act like a real grown-up. In my mind, I made a list of about a million fun things I could do in the deli. All you have to do is turn the page to see a few of them.

CHAPTER 3

A MILLION FUN THINGS I COULD DO IN THE DELI

BY HANK ZIPZER

(Okay, it's not a million, it's four, but I've never been good at math.)

1. Try to scoop potato salad into little paper cups without licking the spoon even once.

2. Squirt smiley faces on the sandwiches with the mustard bottle. (Hey, I could even use a pickle slice for the nose.)

3. See how many sprinkle cookies I can stuff into my mouth when no one is watching. (My record is four and a half. I'm going for five.)

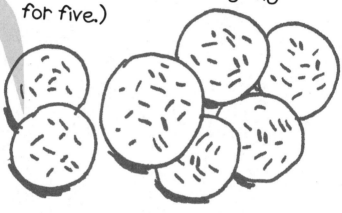

4. Put on a talent show for the customers. (I can't sing. I can't dance. But I can burp my name.)

5. I was starting on Number 5, but I don't know what it is because I fell asleep.

CHAPTER 4

I woke up early the next morning, all excited. I brushed my teeth. I brushed my hair and even put some goop in it like a grown-up. I looked in the mirror to make sure that all the hairs on my head were lying down. They were cooperating. Then I picked out a pair of socks that actually matched. And to finish off the grown-up look, I chose a shirt that had no trace of yesterday's taco lunch on it. When I came out for breakfast, Emily laughed.

"You look like a mini-Dad,"
she said. "Except more dorky."

"You look like a maxi-lizard,"
I shot back. "Except more slimy."

"For your information, Hank,
lizards aren't slimy," Emily replied.
"They are shiny because they
have natural oil in their scales."

"No breakfast for me, Mom," I
called out. "I just lost my appetite."

My mom handed me a slice of
toast with peanut butter, anyway.

"You've got to have something,"
she said. "You need energy for
the busy day ahead."

My dad came rushing into the living room, pulling on his jacket.

"Let's move, folks," he said. "We're running late."

We all gathered our things, headed out the door, and got into the elevator. When we got outside, my dad and Emily headed right to school. My mom and I went the opposite way, toward the Crunchy Pickle.

The place was already buzzing when we got there. Lots of people were sitting in the booths, having breakfast. Some people were waiting in line for an empty table. There was even a crowd at the counter where people were ordering a roll and coffee to take to their offices.

My mom looked around the deli.

I could see that she was feeling great
that we had so many customers.
When she first took over the Crunchy
Pickle from Papa Pete, she wasn't
sure she would be good at running
a deli. But wow, was she wrong.

"We've got to get busy, Hank,"
she said. "It's the breakfast rush."

"Okay, Mom. I'm ready. What
do we do first?"

"I'm going to go wait on the
customers at the counter. I'll put

Carlos in charge of you. Come on, he's over at the grill."

My mom took my hand, and we made our way across the crowd, saying good morning to everyone as we passed. We found Carlos at the grill, flipping turkey sausages. They sizzled on the grill and smelled delicious. I wanted one, but I knew it wasn't right to eat the customers' food.

Carlos, who has worked at the deli since he was a teenager, turned around to say hi. He had a lot of goop in his hair, too. He used it to make his hair stand up in tall spikes, which poked through his hairnet.

He must have seen me checking out his hair.

"I know what you're thinking, Little Man," he said, turning around so I could see the back of his hair, too. "You're thinking my hair is as cool as an iceberg in winter. I couldn't agree more. The reason it's so cool is that I have a hot date with my girl tonight."

"Oh no," I said. "If it's going to be hot, you should take off your sweater."

Carlos stared at me, then burst out laughing.

"You have a lot to learn, Little Man," he said.

"Speaking of which," my mom said, "Hank is going to be spending the day with us. I'd like you to put him to work."

"Sure thing, Mrs. Z.," Carlos said. "It's hopping in here, and we can sure use extra help."

"Good, then I'll leave Hank in your hands."

She gave me a quick kiss, which I hoped no one saw, and hurried off into the crowd of people.

"My mom still kisses me every time I leave the house," Carlos said.

"I ask her not to kiss me in public," I said.

"Moms are like that," Carlos

said, taking the turkey sausages off the grill and sliding them onto a plate. "Come on, Little Man, we've got a lot of breakfast orders to fill."

"What's first?" I asked him with a big smile.

"I'm going to scramble up a pile of eggs to go with these sausages," he said. "Why don't you head over to Table Seven and take their order? They've been waiting a long time. They look hungry."

Carlos handed me a pad of paper and a pencil, and hurried off into the kitchen. The second he was gone, the smile disappeared from my face. I stared at the pad and pencil, and sighed.

Wouldn't you know it? The one
thing I knew I couldn't do was the
one thing I was asked to do first.

I took a deep breath and headed
over to Table Seven. Three men
were sitting there, holding menus
and talking. One had a mustache,
one was bald, and one had a
ponytail. I stood in front of them
with my hands shaking. I hoped with
all my might that they were only
hungry for something I could spell.

CHAPTER 5

I gave the three men my most grown-up smile.

"Hi, I'm Hank," I said. "I'm new here."

The man with the mustache looked up from his menu.

"Kind of short for a waiter, aren't you?" he asked.

"For a second-grader, I'm pretty average," I answered. "Heather Payne is the tallest girl in our class, but most of us are this size. Now, what would you like?"

Mustache Man sighed and shut his menu. "I'll have two eggs over easy, bacon crispy, fruit, no potatoes, and an English muffin, hold the butter," he said.

My ears nearly fell off my head. How was I supposed to write any of that down? I froze. I couldn't even write the word "egg." All that came out of my pencil was an "e."

Okay, Hank, I told myself. *Don't panic. You'll just have to remember their order. You can do that.*

The bald man put his menu down and leaned forward.

"Blueberry waffle, hot raspberry syrup, extra melted butter, and a turkey sausage."

I could feel his words going in through my ears, but they raced around my brain like a pinball. I looked over at the guy with the ponytail, hoping that he was not hungry. But oh was he ever! He wanted lunch for breakfast.

"I'll have your cheeseburger deluxe, extra pickles, Russian dressing on a toasted bun."

Deluxe? I've never even heard that word before. And why would you want to see a Russian person dressing?

The bald man flashed me a smile.

"Look at you, smart kid," he said. "You didn't even have to write any of our order down."

"No, sir, it's all up here,"
I said, pointing to my head.

I dashed over to Carlos to
give him the order, trying to
remember their words.

"Hey, Little Man, I'm busy,"
he said. "I got eight omelets
coming out for Table Eleven.
Give your order to Vlady. He'll
take care of you."

Vlady is a big man with so
much hair on his arms, his skin
looks like he's wearing a sweater.
I've known him since I was little.

"Vlady," I said. "You have to
listen to me fast before I forget
everything."

In a giant rush of words, the
order came spilling out of my mouth.

"Slow down, Small Fry," Vlady said. That might be insulting coming from anyone else, but next to him, everyone is a small fry.

"I can't slow down," I told him, "or I'm going to forget the whole order."

Vlady listened and jotted down some notes.

"Strange order," he said. "But your mother says the customer is always right."

He shrugged, then turned to the griddle and started to cook.

"I've got a lot of orders coming in," he said. "You could really help me out by going back to the table and making sure their water glasses are full."

I grabbed a pitcher of ice water. I had to use both hands because it was heavy. Holding it against my chest, I made my way over to Table Seven without spilling a drop. I was starting to get the hang of this waiter thing! I was also starting to have a frozen chest.

"More water, anyone?" I asked the men.

"Sure, that would be great," the man with the mustache answered, barely stopping the joke he was telling to the others.

His glass was pretty high up, and I was pretty low down. I stood on my tiptoes and pulled the glass to the edge of the table so I could reach it better. I lifted the pitcher with both hands and started to pour. Unfortunately, there was no glass in the area

I was pouring. Water spilled out onto the table and dripped off the edge and into the man's lap.

He jumped up from his chair and screamed like he had seen a mouse.

"I'm s-so s-sorry, s-sir," I stammered. "I guess being a waiter isn't as easy as it looks."

"Don't worry about it, kid," the man with the mustache said, picking up his napkin and dabbing at his pants. "Every waiter is allowed one mistake."

The other men were laughing. I was so glad they weren't angry.

"Just go see how our food is coming along," the guy with the ponytail said to me.

"Good idea," I answered. "I'll leave the pitcher here so you can pour your own water."

"Good idea yourself," he said with a laugh.

I hurried away before I could get into more trouble. I looked around for my mom to see if she had noticed, but she was in the back of the deli talking to a delivery man. I was glad she hadn't seen the mess I had made with the pitcher. I would have been so embarrassed.

I headed over to Vlady to see if the order was ready. He was just finishing putting the food on the plates.

"Let me help you carry this to the table, Small Fry," he said. "You take one plate and I'll carry two."

As I hurried across the restaurant carrying the plate, I felt so proud. This was my first order ever. I set it down on the

table in front of the bald man.
Then I took each of the next two
plates from Vlady and set them
down in front of the others. Vlady
went back to the griddle, and I
just stood there with a huge smile
spread across my face.

"I hope you enjoy your meal,"
I said to them.

The men were staring at their
plates.

"Why are there blueberries on
my cheeseburger?" the man with
the ponytail asked.

"And pickles on my waffle?"
the bald man chimed in.

"And hot raspberry syrup on
my fried eggs?" the man with the
mustache said.

Uh-oh. This was not sounding good. I had told Vlady the right food, but in the wrong place.

"Um . . . um . . . We like to surprise our customers," I said at last. "We make up our own combinations. It's what we here at the Crunchy Pickle call creative cooking."

"It's what I call horrible cooking," the man with the mustache said. "I can't eat this."

"Me either," said the man with the ponytail. "A blueberry cheeseburger is disgusting."

"Waffles with pickle juice will give me a stomachache," the bald man said. "This food has to go back."

"Couldn't we just keep this little problem between us guys?" I whispered.

"We can't pay for this," the man with the ponytail said. "We need to see the manager."

"That would be my mom," I answered with a gulp. "She's very busy right now."

"Well, you tell her we need to speak with her," Mustache Man said. "We've been customers here for a long time, and we've never had a bad meal."

This was worse than I thought. I was in big trouble. Not only did I mess up, I messed up with my mom's best customers. I looked over at the counter and saw her handing a to-go cup of coffee to a man in a white shirt. She looked so happy. I think she could feel me looking at her, because she caught my eye and flashed me a big smile.

My stomach was suddenly full
of butterflies.

I knew that smile wasn't
going to last long.

CHAPTER 6

"Mom," I said, walking up to her. "I want you to stay calm."

"I don't like the sound of this," she said.

She put down the coffee pot and put her hands on my shoulders.

"You look so serious," she said. "Last time I saw that look, you left the front door open and Cheerio ran away. Remember, we had to spend the whole afternoon searching the apartment building until we found him."

"Yeah, but it was so cute when we found him in the laundry room, all curled up in Mrs. Fink's warm clothes right out of the dryer," I said. "Her sweat socks were hanging off his ears. You've got to admit that was funny, Mom."

I tried to laugh and hoped my mom would, too.

"Hank," she said, not laughing even a little, "you can't turn everything into a joke. This is my business, and we have to take it seriously. So just tell me what happened."

"It's about those men at Table Seven. They want to see you. I kind of messed up their order a little tiny bit."

"How tiny is a little bit?"

"Let's just say there was pickle juice on their waffles."

"Oh, this isn't good." She shook her head.

"And blueberries on the cheeseburger. I thought I told Vlady the right order, but . . ."

She didn't even let me finish. She just spun around and marched right over to the men. I hid behind the bagel counter as I watched her talking to them.

Her hands were flying all over
the place, and I knew she was
apologizing. My mom is so good at
talking with people, I was sure she
could make the men understand.
I was positive—right up to the
moment they grabbed their jackets
and walked out without paying.
My mom was frowning as she
walked back to me.

"How did it go?" I asked
hopefully.

"It went well for the diner
down the block," she said.
"That's where they're going."

"Oh, Mom, I'm so sorry," I
said. "It's my fault. You don't
have to give me my allowance
for the next three weeks."

"Hank, how did this happen?" she asked.

"Those three men all wanted a lot of food," I said, the words just pouring out of my mouth. "And I couldn't write it down quickly enough and even if I could, I didn't know how to spell a lot of the words like 'syrup' or 'sausage.' So I tried to remember it all in my head, but my head didn't cooperate and got it all mixed up."

"I understand, but what you did was wrong," she said. "If you knew you couldn't remember the order, you should have asked for help. If you know you can't do something, don't try to hide it. Just ask for help."

That was easy for her to say. She almost never has to ask for help. There are so many things I can't do that I would be asking for help every two seconds. And that's embarrassing.

Just then, the front door of the deli swung open, and my grandfather, Papa Pete, burst in. He was wearing his favorite red sweat suit that makes him look like a giant strawberry.

"Oh, here's my favorite grandson," he said, giving me a bear hug.

"I'm your only grandson, Papa Pete."

"Which is exactly why you're my favorite," he said, and let out a big laugh. That laugh changed my whole mood.

"Hank is working here today," my mom said. "And we're looking for a job he'd be comfortable doing."

"I know exactly what Hank should do," Papa Pete said. "I used to run this place, remember? And not to brag, but I was known as the King of the Triple-Decker Sandwich. How would you like to learn how to make one, Hankie?"

"Could I, Mom?" I asked.

"Sure," she said. "That sounds like a good job for you. I'll be busy filling the order for the Teacher Appreciation Dinner. So Papa Pete is in charge of you."

"Don't worry about Hankie and me," Papa Pete said. Then, turning to me, he added, "Step into my office, youngster, and I'll teach you the tricks of the trade."

I followed Papa Pete over to the sandwich-making area, where Vlady and Carlos were just starting to prepare for the lunch rush.

"Vlady, my good man," Papa

Pete said, slapping him on the back. "Nice to see you."

"Welcome back, Papa Pete," Vlady said. "We miss you around here."

"Yeah," Carlos chimed in. "There's no one to give me advice about girls, except Vlady. Last week, he told me that instead of bringing my date flowers, I should bring her a pint of radishes in sour cream."

"How did that work out for you?" Papa Pete asked.

"It was a very short date," Carlos said. "I got to her house at seven and was on the subway heading home by seven thirty."

"Well, if you gentlemen will give us some room," Papa Pete said, "I'm about to teach my grandson the secrets of the triple-decker sandwich."

We hardly had any time to get started on our lesson, because a customer came hurrying up to the sandwich counter. It was Bruce, who delivers mail to the buildings in our neighborhood.

"Hi, guys," Bruce said. "I delivered so much mail this

morning, I worked up quite an appetite. Can you get me a salami, cheese, fried-egg triple-decker as fast as you can?"

"Papa Pete, can you take this?" Carlos asked. "I'm going to go wipe down the tables for lunch."

"And I'll go help the people in the booth by the window," Vlady said. "They look hungry."

Papa Pete and I got busy on Bruce's triple-decker sandwich.

Putting the salami and cheese on the bread was pretty easy. The fried egg part was tricky.

"Hankie, bring me an egg," Papa Pete said, dropping a blob of butter on the grill.

I went to the bowl where we keep the eggs and picked one up. I reached out to hand it to Papa Pete, but I let it go before he grabbed it. We both watched the egg fall through the air and land splat on his shoes. Papa Pete didn't even get mad.

"That's okay," he said, wiping the egg yolk off his shoes. "This is going to make my shoes so shiny, they'll glow in the dark."

Papa Pete fried up a new egg, and let me scoop it onto the sandwich and stick a toothpick in each half to hold it together. We handed it to Bruce, and before he even reached the cash register to pay, we had another customer. It was Lanni, who worked at the nail salon down the block.

"How about a nice triple-decker for you," Papa Pete said. "I got some rare roast beef right here."

"I don't eat meat," Lanni said.

"How about a fried egg sandwich?" I suggested to her. "I just learned how to handle that."

"Okay," she said. "On wheat bread."

This time when I took the eggs out of the bowl, I made sure to put them directly into Papa Pete's hand. I was really catching on to this sandwich work. I did have a little problem sticking the toothpick into each half. I kind of forgot that egg yolks can drip all over the rest of the sandwich. But Papa Pete said that's what egg yolks are supposed to do.

After Lanni left, the line got

even longer at the sandwich counter. Carlos and Vlady came over to help until my mom showed up, looking stressed.

"I need your help," she said to Papa Pete. "The meat slicing machine is acting up. Can you come take a look at it? It needs your special touch."

"Do you want my help, too, Mom?" I asked.

"The early lunch customers are coming in right now," she said. "You would be a big help staying right here and making sandwiches with Carlos and Vlady."

"Great, I'm pretty expert at making sandwiches now," I said.

"You're going to have to

concentrate, Hank. Lunchtime is really busy here."

That sounded exciting. I could already see myself standing in between Carlos and Vlady, passing sliced roast beef to my right and salami to my left. Or maybe it was the other way around. I can never get that left and right thing left. I mean right.

Papa Pete and my mom hurried to the back room of the deli, and I took my place at the sandwich counter.

Bring on the crowds, I thought to myself. *Hank Zipzer is on the case!*

My mind must be really good

at magic, because as soon as I had that thought, presto, the front door swung open with our next customers.

Uh-oh, my mind must have used some bad magic, because standing there at the front door was a stink bomb in human form.

CHAPTER 7

The stink bomb's name was Nick McKelty. He was with his dad, who had a really unhappy look on his face. I couldn't blame him. I would have that same look, too, if I had to spend an entire day with Nick the Tick.

Carlos was busy making a ham and cheese sandwich.

"Do me a favor, Little Man," he said. "Go seat those people and give them a menu."

Oh no. I was going to have

to wait on Nick McKelty? I'd rather ski down Mount Everest naked. In a blizzard.

"I see that Table Seven is empty," Carlos said. "Seat them there."

Double oh no. Table Seven! Bad things happen there. That was definitely not my lucky table.

"How about if I finish the sandwich, and you show them to the table?" I suggested.

"No can do," he said. "You can't use the knife. Mom's orders."

I picked up two menus and walked as slowly as I could toward the front door. When McKelty saw me, he burst out laughing.

"What a boring job, handing out menus," he whispered in my ear.

"Thanks, Nick. It's nice to see you, too," I whispered back. "I thought you'd be spraying anti-stink stuff into bowling shoes."

"Hello, Hank," Nick's father said. "I see you're helping your mom on Take Your Child to Work Day. Nick and I were at the bowling alley having a fun day, too, until the automatic pinsetter broke. We thought we'd grab some lunch while they're fixing it."

"Let me show you to your table," I said.

"Really? You can do that?" Nick snorted. "Aren't you the one who always gets lost?"

I didn't answer, just made my way over to Table Seven. I wanted to stick my foot out and trip the big creep, but I knew that wouldn't be right.

"Is this the best table you have?" Nick asked. "It's too close to the door."

On second thought, I should have tripped him.

Mr. McKelty didn't look pleased with his son.

"This table is just fine, Hank," he said to me. "I'm sure Nick would agree. Don't you, Nick?"

"Fine, let's just order," Nick said, taking a seat. "What do you have that's any good?"

"Everything on the menu," I answered. "But today we're making some pretty great triple-deckers."

"Sounds fabulous," Mr. McKelty said. "We'll each take one. Why don't you surprise us with your best combinations."

As I walked back to Carlos,

I thought about what I'd like to make for Nick's special sandwich. I came up with onion, mustard, crushed shrimp shells, and day-old baloney piled high on stale bread. Oh, and don't let me forget the moldy cheese.

I gave my suggestion to Carlos, but he just laughed.

"What do you have against those people?" he said.

"Mr. McKelty is really nice," I said. "But his son Nick is the class bully. And the person he likes to bully most is me."

"I see where you're coming from," Carlos said. "But remember, we're the Crunchy Pickle. And we have a reputation to protect. You know our motto: *Our sandwiches are almost too good to eat.*"

"You're right," I said. "Besides, maybe one of our delicious sandwiches will put Nick in a better mood."

"I like the way you're thinking, Little Man," Carlos said. "So what do you say we make your pal a nice pastrami, Swiss cheese, and coleslaw triple-decker. We'll make his dad a roast beef, cheddar cheese, and coleslaw. I have to go get some fresh rye bread. While I'm gone, you can get me that sliced pastrami over there on the wax paper."

That seemed easy enough. The piled-up pastrami was just a few feet away, sitting on the counter waiting for me. The walk over to it was smooth sailing. Three, maybe four steps. Picking it up was no problem. I grabbed the wax paper from the bottom. I could feel the steamy warmth of the pastrami against the palm of my hand. I leaned over and took a big whiff. Man, did it smell delicious.

That was the exact moment I realized that I can't smell and watch where I'm going at the same time. I didn't notice that there was a slice of tomato that had dropped onto the floor. My feet went sliding out from under me, and the pastrami left my hands, all on its own, and decided to land on the floor.

As I looked down at the pastrami that was supposed to be in Nick McKelty's sandwich, I thought of all the things I could do with it. The list that popped into my head made me laugh out loud.

CHAPTER 8

FOUR THINGS I COULD DO WITH NICK THE TICK'S PASTRAMI PILE

BY HANK ZIPZER

1. I could tell Carlos that I dropped it and he would slice a new pile.

2. I could step on it with my sneaker and grind it around a little bit before putting it on his sandwich.

3. I could pick it up, throw it back down again, and then put it on his sandwich.

4. I could pick it up, wash it off, pat it dry, then put it on his sandwich.

Which of these four things do you think I did?

CHAPTER 9

As much as I wanted to squish the pastrami with my sneaker and then serve it to Nick, a little voice inside me said, *You can't do that at your mom's restaurant.* You don't know my mom, but she's a clean freak. At home, she vacuums under the couch first thing in the morning and last thing at night. Those poor dust balls never even have a chance to get to know one another under there.

That same little voice inside

didn't stop there. It went on to say that squishing the pastrami under my feet would be a really mean thing to do. That little voice had so much to say that I decided I had better listen to it.

I bent down and picked up the pile of pastrami and plopped it back on the wax paper. I wiped off as much of the tomato slime as I could and walked over to the sink. I turned on the water, not too hot and not too cold. Then I held the pastrami under it. To be sure I got it really clean, I added just one tiny drop of liquid soap. There were two bottles of soap there. One smelled like coconuts. The other smelled like roses. I picked the coconut one.

I thought it would give the pastrami a nice fruity touch.

Let me just say this. It's amazing how many bubbles one little drop of soap can make. The pastrami looked like it swallowed a bubble maker. I quickly looked over my shoulder to see if Carlos was on his way back. He was! As fast as I could, I rinsed the bubbles off one more time and tossed the meat onto a paper towel to dry it.

"Hey, Little Man," Carlos said, looking at the paper towel. "You don't have to dry off our pastrami. People like it when it's juicy."

"Oh, then McKelty's going to love this pile," I said.

Carlos made the two triple-decker sandwiches in no time. On Nick's, he piled on my pastrami, a glob of coleslaw, and some Swiss cheese. On Mr. McKelty's sandwich, he put roast beef, cheddar cheese, and another glob of coleslaw. Dropping two pickles on each of the plates, he said, "If you carry one, I'll take the other. Teamwork, Little Man, that's what it's all about."

Carlos handed me the plate with Nick's sandwich, and he took Mr. McKelty's. As we crossed the restaurant, I glanced down at Nick's sandwich. I thought that I

saw a tiny bubble
squirting out
from the meat.

   *Could it be?
No, not possible.*
I rinsed that pastrami really well.
At least I think I did. I hope I did.
I'm sure I did. Well, pretty sure.

   "Here you go, gentlemen,"
Carlos said to the McKeltys as he
slid his plate onto the table. "The
best-looking sandwiches in the city.
From, if I do say so myself, two of
the best-looking guys in the city."

   Carlos tapped the top of his
spiky hair and flashed a confident
smile. Mr. McKelty let out a
friendly laugh. Then he picked up
his sandwich.

"I can't wait to dig in to this beauty," he said.

Nick the Tick had already dug in to his. Even though his mouth is the size of a dinosaur cave, he could only fit in two out of the three layers. One of them was the pastrami layer. I held my breath while he started to chew. All of a sudden, he wrinkled up his nose, his mouth, and then his entire face. He looked like the raisin you leave behind in your cereal bowl.

"Ugh," he said, spitting some pastrami into his hand. "This meat tastes like coconuts."

As he spoke, a thin bubble flew out

of his mouth and popped in the air.

"Coconuts?" Carlos said with a laugh. "You've got some imagination, kid." Carlos turned to Mr. McKelty. "How's the roast beef?"

"Tastes like roast beef to me," Mr. McKelty answered.

"That's what I'm talking about," Carlos said.

While they were chatting, I glanced back at Nick to see more bubbles drift out of his mouth.

"What did you put in here, Zipperhead?" McKelty said. "This is the worst sandwich I've ever had."

He threw the sandwich down
onto the table, missing the plate
entirely.

"Nick!" his father said. "That
is a very rude thing to do."

"I agree with you," Carlos said.
"I'm riding the same train you are."

Nick stood up, picked up his
napkin, and spit out what was
in his mouth.

"That's what I think of your
sandwich," he said, staring at me.
A little drool slid down the side of
his mouth.

"That's it," Mr. McKelty said.
"Even if you don't like the taste
of your sandwich, this is not the
way we behave in a restaurant.
May we just have our bill, please?

Obviously my son needs a lesson in manners before we go out to lunch again."

Carlos grabbed the plates and went back to the counter to prepare the bill. McKelty frowned at me, but I just gave him the old Zipzer smile.

As I turned to walk away, I could hear his father saying, "That Hank's a nice boy. You two should be friends. You could learn a few things from him."

"Yeah, like how to flunk a spelling test," McKelty said. "He's great at that."

Normally, a comment like that would hurt my feelings. But this time, it didn't. I had the last laugh.

CHAPTER 10

By three o'clock that afternoon, I was so tired, all I wanted was to lie down and take a nap. I snuck over to one of the empty booths and flopped down. I was all curled up on the leather, ready to drop off into dreamland, when I felt someone shaking my shoulder.

It was Frankie and Ashley.

"Hey, what are you guys doing here?" I yawned.

"My dad dropped us off so we could see how your day is going,"

87

Frankie said. "We could even help out, if you want, and then all walk home together."

"Looks like you could use some help," Ashley said. "You look pooped."

"I worked hard," I said. "How about you guys?"

"I had such a fun day," Frankie said. "I did a magic trick for my dad's students."

"Did you pull a washcloth out of the top hat?" I asked him.

"Yes I did. But the biggest hit of the day was when I pulled a scarf out of my nose."

"Eww, that sounds painful," Ashley said.

We all cracked up.

"My day was really fun, too," Ashley told us. "I passed out lunch trays and apple juice to so many nice people. Mrs. Ruiz in Room 227 taught me how to make a red-and-white fairy wand out of a plastic straw. I hope she gets better soon."

"Me too," I said. "Now can I go back to sleep?"

"No you can't," a voice said.

It was my mom, who had come out from the kitchen. "I really need your help, Hank," she went on. "And I'm glad you two showed up, too. We're going to need all the help we can get to finish the platters in time so your teachers can have a good dinner."

"That sounds exciting," Ashley said.

"I'm in," Frankie agreed.

"Great. Go into my office and call your parents. Tell them Papa Pete will bring you home after we drop off the food at school. Hank, let's get you busy with the potato salad."

"I'm on it, Mom. Just one thing. I have no idea how to make potato salad."

"It's already made," she said. "You just have to scoop it into a big bowl and sprinkle some parsley on top."

"I'm on it, Mom. Oh, by the way, what's parsley?"

My mom sighed.

"Come on, let's go find Papa Pete in the back room," she said. "He'll explain it all to you."

The back room was as busy as a beehive. Everybody was working as fast as they could. Papa Pete was stacking the meat platters. Vlady was in charge of the cheese. Carlos was arranging different kinds of bread in a circle on the tray.

"Papa Pete," my mom called out. "Please show Hank how to add the finishing touches to the potato salad. Frankie and Ashley will be in to help as soon as they're off the phone. I'll take care of any customers out front while you guys load the minivan."

Papa Pete gave me an ice-cream scooper.

"This is what we use to scoop the potato salad into the serving bowl," he explained. "Make sure the bowl is nice and full, then sprinkle some chopped parsley on top. That's the green stuff in this baggie."

I looked at the baggie and saw little bunches of a leafy green thing. I recognized it right away.

"Ohhhhhh, so that's parsley,"
I said. "I thought it was just called
'the green stuff on the side of the
plate that no one eats.'"

Papa Pete burst out laughing
and gave me a big hug.

"That's my Hankie," he said. "You
always see things your own way!"

Frankie and Ashley hurried in
and got busy. Ashley put the pickles
around the meat platter. She loves
to do art projects,
so she arranged
the pickles to look
like the meat was
wearing a skirt.

Frankie was put in charge of
squirting mustard and ketchup from
big bottles into smaller serving

bowls. Every time he squirted one of the bottles, it made a farting sound. And every time it did that, we burst out laughing.

"Hey, people," Carlos said. "One day you'll learn that laughing at fart sounds is definitely uncool."

"But it's so funny," we told him.

"Maybe when you're nine," he said. "But you better grow out of that, or you're going to have trouble getting a date on Saturday nights."

We just looked at one another and wondered what he was talking about. Who wants a date on Saturday night? It's much more fun to build a pillow fort on the couch and watch a monster movie.

Papa Pete said it was time to load the minivan.

"We have to move fast, folks," he said. "We have just enough time to get to PS 87."

Everyone grabbed their tray or bowl, and raced into the alley where the minivan was parked. We handed each plate of food to Papa Pete, who slid them onto the shelves in the back of the van. Moving quickly, he pulled a bright red bungee cord across each shelf so the food would stay right where he put it.

"Who's coming with me to deliver this?" Papa Pete called out.

"We are!" I cried.

I looked over at Frankie and Ashley, and they nodded their heads as fast as they could.

We all piled in the back seat and had our safety belts on in no time. Carlos jumped into the passenger side. Papa Pete looked at his watch as he climbed in behind the wheel.

"It's going to be tight," he said.

"I'm counting on you to get us there in time," Carlos said. "And to get us out of there, too. I have a hot date."

"I'll try my best," said Papa Pete.

We pulled out of the alley onto 77th Street and turned onto Broadway with no problem—until we reached a huge cement mixer that was stopped in the middle of the street. It was totally blocking us. Papa Pete leaned out of the window to see what was going on.

"I think that truck is trying to turn around," he said, "but he doesn't have room to back up."

"Can we take another street?" I asked.

Papa Pete turned and looked out the back window. There were cars lined up behind us as far as you could see.

"We're boxed in," Papa Pete said. "There's nothing we can do but wait."

Frankie looked at his watch.

"Not to stress you out or anything, Papa Pete, but we're now officially late," he said.

"Maybe this isn't the time to point that out, dude," Carlos whispered to him.

"This could take forever," Papa Pete muttered.

"I hope the teachers don't leave," I said.

"Shhh," Ashley said to me. "You're not helping."

That monster truck was not going anywhere soon. There we were, like Santa Claus on Christmas with a sleigh full of goodies, and we were stuck at the North Pole.

CHAPTER 11

04:17

If you've never been in a traffic jam in New York City, let me tell you this: It's really loud. Everybody honks their horn at the same time, hoping that the car in front of them will move. But it never does, because it has no place to go, either. We spent fifteen minutes listening to everyone honking at the cement mixer.

Papa Pete doesn't believe in honking, but he does believe in shouting. He stuck half his body out the window, trying to explain our situation.

"Hey, buddy," he called out to the driver. "I've got hungry teachers waiting. You've got to get a move on."

"I'm trying, Pops," the driver said. "Just got to back this buggy up a few more inches so I can make the turn. Oh, and say hi to the teachers for me. My wife is a teacher."

By the time we got to PS 87, it was seventeen minutes after four o'clock. I knew that from reading the digital clock on the dashboard in Papa Pete's van. I still can't read a regular clock very well. If you ask me, the little hand isn't so little, and the big hand isn't so big. In other words, they both look the same to me.

The Teacher Appreciation Dinner was in the multipurpose room. It's a really good thing it's on the first floor so we didn't have to go up any steps. We were all carrying a lot of stuff. My job was to carry the bowl of potato salad. Ashley had the coleslaw, and Frankie got the easy job of taking the ketchup and mustard bowls. Papa Pete carried the meat platter and Carlos took the cheese platter.

"You lead the way, Hankie," Papa Pete said. "We're right behind you."

We passed Principal Love's
office, the nurse's office, and the
bulletin board with the kindergarten
class's self-portraits. They all
looked like they had arms growing
out of their ears. I wanted to laugh,
but I stopped myself because I
didn't want to take any chances on
dropping the potato salad.

When we got to the end of the
hall, I saw that the doors to the
multipurpose room were open. There
were lots of teachers inside, sitting

on both sides of a long table. They were drinking fruit punch. At one end of the table there were plates all stacked up, looking empty and lonely. As usual, Principal Love was talking, probably giving one of his long, long speeches. I noticed a few of the teachers were yawning, which is what I always do when he talks.

"Dinner has arrived," Papa Pete shouted out. "We're here to tickle your taste buds."

"Well, bring it in, folks," Principal Love said. "As I always say, put good food and an empty plate together and you get a plateful of good food."

No one ever understands what Principal Love says or why he says it, but the teachers were too hungry to care. When they saw us coming in with all the platters, they burst into applause. It felt great to make them so happy. I looked around the room and saw Ms. Flowers applauding the loudest. She gave me that big Ms. Flowers smile that makes you feel so good. Then she waved.

"Hi, Hank," she called out. "Hi, Frankie and Ashley."

"Hi, Ms. Flowers," I called back.

I should have stopped right there, but I didn't. I took my hand off the bowl of potato salad and waved back at her.

Hank, WHAT were you thinking?

The bowl of potato salad slipped out of my arms. I tried to catch it in midair to keep it from falling. But that didn't work. In fact, just the opposite happened. My hands hit it like a volleyball, and it sailed even higher into the air. We learned in our science unit that whatever goes up, must come down. And I'm here to say, that goes double for potato salad!

CHAPTER 12

Every bit of the potato salad—including the chopped parsley—flew out of the bowl like it was a jet plane. When it hit the floor, it splattered all over and made a slippery, goopy carpet. After that, everything happened very quickly. Ashley, who was following right behind me, stepped smack in the middle of the potato salad. Her bowl of coleslaw flew up in the air and landed with a splat on top of the potato salad. Behind her was Frankie. You guessed it. His ketchup and mustard added color to the potato salad mountain that was rising up on the floor. Then Carlos stepped right in the middle of the mess and slid around like he was ice skating.

"Whoa," I heard him shout. "I'm going down."

And with that, his legs flew out from under him, and he plopped down right on his butt. His pants, which were black, were suddenly yellow, red, white, and creamy. His first reaction was to reach up and touch his spiky hair.

"Did I get any potato salad in my hair?" he asked.

Papa Pete was right behind

Carlos with the meat platter.
Luckily, he didn't fall down—but
the salami did. A pile of it landed
right on Carlos's head. It looked
like he was wearing a meat hat.

"I can't go on a date like this!"
he shouted. "I look like a walking
deli sandwich."

Carlos wasn't the only one who
was upset. I stared at the mess on
the floor and realized I had just
ruined the teachers' party. Why
didn't I remember that carrying a

big bowl of potato salad takes two hands? This kind of thing happens to me a lot. I'm always in the middle of trouble, and I never know how I got there.

The teachers just stood there with their mouths hanging open. This wasn't the kind of mess you could fix with a couple of paper towels. This was going to take a shovel.

Principal Love was on his feet. The mole on his cheek, which looks like the Statue of Liberty without the torch, was bouncing up and down like it was on a trampoline.

"Look what you've done, Hank Zipzer," he shouted. "Instead of giving your teachers a delicious meal, you've created a sloppy mess."

I have never been so embarrassed in my life. My face turned as red as the ketchup that was all over my shoes.

"I'm sorry," I said. "I was just trying to wave hello."

"You never think before you act," he said.

"Whoa, that's harsh," Carlos said.

Papa Pete put down the half-empty meat tray and walked over to Principal Love.

"What do you think he's going to say?" Ashley whispered to me.

"I don't know, but I hope I don't get into more trouble."

"Don't worry," Frankie said. "Papa Pete will handle this. He never lets us down."

"Excuse me," Papa Pete said to Principal Love. His voice was very calm. "What happened here was an accident."

"And I'm so sorry about it," I said. "It was all my fault."

"It was an accident, Hankie," Papa Pete said. "It isn't anyone's fault. That's why they call them accidents."

"Nonsense," a teacher named Ms. Adolf said. Everyone in school knows that she's the meanest teacher we have. "I saw what happened with my very eyes. That boy was careless."

"My grandson Hank is a very thoughtful person. Sometimes he gets excited and that causes problems. But he always tries his hardest to do the right thing."

"I agree," Ms. Flowers said. "Hank is always the first one in my class to raise his hand when I ask for help."

"And he tries very hard in my music class," Mr. Rock said. "He plays the triangle with all his heart."

Principal Love still seemed angry. His mole looked like it was doing the hula.

"Do you consider this a party," he grumbled to Papa Pete, "with most of the food on the floor?"

"I just happen to have several trays of black and white cookies in the van," Papa Pete said. "How about if I bring those up?"

"Oh, that's my favorite kind of cookie," Ms. Flowers said. A lot of the teachers agreed.

"Me too!" I said. "Hey, I have an idea. We can have a reverse dinner! We'll have dessert first."

"Good thinking, Hankie," Papa Pete said. "While everyone is enjoying the cookies, Carlos and I will go back to the deli and bring some meatloaf and macaroni and cheese. We already prepared it for the dinner crowd."

"Let me remind you, Carlos has a hot date," Carlos said, shaking his head.

"Come on, Carlos," I whispered to him. "I really need you to do this for me."

"Okay, Little Man," he said. "I'm going to do this for you. But if my girlfriend, Ramona, doesn't talk to me again because I'm late, you've got to call her and explain."

"No problem there," Frankie told Carlos. "Hank can talk his way out of anything."

"Yeah, he's got a magical mouth," Ashley chimed in.

"This is certainly not the Teacher Appreciation Dinner we had planned," Principal Love said. "A dessert-first dinner is a very strange way to let your teachers know how much you appreciate them."

"Actually, Principal Love," Ms. Flowers said, "I find this a very creative way to say thank you to us. Everyone loves cookies, don't we?"

All the teachers nodded in agreement.

"And Hank's idea to have
a reverse dinner is very original.
It shows that his mind is always
working."

I felt so good when she said
that out loud to everyone that
my mouth opened all by itself,
without my brain even telling it
to. And this is what came out.

"Ms. Flowers, you are the best
second-grade teacher in the whole
world," I said. "No matter what

mistake I make, you're always the first one to understand. You never make me feel stupid just because I can't spell or do math. And you teach me lots of interesting stuff, like if you lift a kangaroo's tail off the ground, it can't hop."

Everybody burst out laughing. Everybody but Ms. Flowers. She stood up and came over to me.

"Hank," she said, "you have just given me the best Teacher Appreciation Dinner any teacher could wish for."

"Even if the potato salad is all over the floor?" I said.

"Yes, even then. What's a little mess compared to the wonderful feelings you just expressed?"

"Whoa," Carlos said. "I think I'm going to cry—and it's not good to show up on a date with watery eyes."

Everybody smiled. I think I might have even seen a mini-smile on Principal Love's face.

"You're a great kid," Mr. Rock called out.

"That remains to be seen," Ms. Adolf said. "Wait until he gets to my fourth-grade class. Then we'll see how great he is."

Just the sound of her voice made me shake in my sneakers.

"Hank," Ms. Flowers said. "I so appreciate your appreciation. You remind me why being a teacher is such a great job. You have a good heart, and that's what I appreciate most about you."

And even though I had made a big mistake with the potato salad, all the teachers stood up and applauded for me.

Wow, that was a surprise. I never expected that the Teacher Appreciation Dinner would turn into a Student Appreciation Dinner, too—potato salad and all.

CHAPTER 13

FIVE THINGS I LEARNED FROM TAKE YOUR CHILD TO WORK DAY

BY HANK ZIPZER

1. Never wave while you're carrying a bowl of potato salad.

2. If you're washing a pile of pastrami, DON'T use soap.

3. Be nice to the person who's taking your order in a restaurant. Maybe they have trouble spelling, just like me.

4. Customers don't like it when you take a bite of their pickle before they do.

5. Going to work is hard work.